Pioneer Ghost

a story of
The Nomadic Ghost

Larry Danek

Day One

The Civil War had ended, and the railroad was under construction but wouldn't be finished for a couple of years. The only way to get to the west coast was to go by horse or wagon train. He had paid the wagon master—the trail boss, as the hired hands called him—to help him get to Oregon.

It was dark, and I felt the pain of the body I just took over. Hunger and thirst were there, but more. It was the ravaging of a small body under the wear and tear it had just been through. The boy had been left behind by the wagon train as it headed out along the Oregon Trail. Somewhere up ahead, the group of travelers had set up camp for the night, and I had to get this body there before they bedded down. I pushed against the walls of the body and issued orders for it to get on the move.

It was reluctant at first and fought me as I pulled to a standing position. "Move one foot ahead and balance to keep from falling over," I said to the clouded brain. The recognition that I was walking took hold, and I set one foot in front of the other. This body had almost reached them before it collapsed in a wagon rut. I managed to drive the body into the encampment.

They had been expecting me, and I was soon eating a large bowl of stew and washing it down with tepid water. A couple of the boys who had taunted me since we left Independence were back at it. "Look! The sickling has caught up to us again."

They didn't persist as one of the women shooed them away. By the time I finished my stew, it was too late to do anything but sleep. I crawled under the tongue of a prairie schooner and put the body in sleep mode. This was a big group, with forty wagons and several hundred people. There were only a couple of Conestogas, and the rest were prairie schooners. He had learned that while waiting for this wagon train to start out. We were a week behind the previous one, and another would be leaving in two weeks. If I fall behind, I might be able to catch the next one when it gets this far.

I knew this would be my last chance to hook up with someone on the train, but this body was done walking for now. I ghosted out to see if I could find someone to accept me. Still, everyone seemed to have already made up their mind about being responsible for another mouth to feed and take care of. I know who I am and wondered why I had this weak little body. I, *The Nomadic Ghost*, am called by the deceased to remedy their situations. If I was called here to remove someone from this wagon train, I might need some assistance. In the morning, I will ask but not beg for a little help.

Day Two

The rest and food had helped a little, and I was up early with the women as they scrambled eggs and fried salt pork. I managed to get a plateful before the others got moving around. Two of the bigger boys found me, pushed me down, and took the plate of food I had almost finished.

"Go hide under a wagon," said one of the boys as they headed over to the cook fire.

I thanked the powers that be, my fellow ghosts, for making sure I got two good meals before the outfit departed. I found one of the trail hands and said, "No one will accept me, and I might have to wait for the next group coming along. Can you get me a gun and some bullets?"

"Kid, you might shoot yourself."

"Gee, I hadn't thought of that, but it might be better than starving to death out here on the prairie all alone."

"I was only kidding. Everyone knows you are having trouble keeping up. Do you know how to use a gun?"

"Yeah, I've seen it done enough times." I couldn't tell him I had used lots of guns in my past lives. Now, why did I remember?

He left to see if anyone had an extra handgun and bullets and returned a few minutes later. "Here, now show me you know how to load it and cock it."

I took the Smith & Wesson forty-four from him and checked to see if it was loaded. It was almost too heavy for this body to handle, but I spun the cylinder and flipped it open, snapped it shut, and pointed it at one of the oxen being hooked up to a Conestoga wagon.

I had to use my left hand to cock the hammer back and then let it fall on an empty chamber. I opened it up again and dropped six rim-fire cartridges in the cylinder. It wasn't a new gun but would work for what I would need. I counted the bullets and said, "Thank you, sir." There were twenty-five rounds in a waterproof bag.

"Are you going to try to keep up today?" he asked.

"I don't think I have it in me to go those next miles. I need some rest and will probably try to hook up with the next group coming along."

I could see he wanted to offer a ride, but I cut it off. "No thanks, you have enough to worry about without caring for me also." The horse might not notice the extra weight, but it could affect his concentration. We were in Indian territory.

Attrition was one thing that happened over the 2,000-mile trek, and people didn't always get where they wanted to go. We had already seen some excess baggage along the trail, but no one stopped to look at it. I had seen two crosses and everyone on this train thought I would be joining those before long. There just might not be anyone to put up the cross.

I left the train early and headed north off the trail. I could see some foliage a mile or two in that direction and thought it might supply me with cover and food. I checked my meager supplies—one handgun, twenty-five bullets, a knife I got from my parents before leaving, and a small bag with a flint in it. I had lost all the other things this body had left Independence with. The brain was foggy enough that I had trouble remembering everything. I was still working on the name I had with this body. John Vanderwick seemed hard to pronounce, so I let it go for a while. My father had major financial losses, and we left Rhode Island to avoid a prison sentence for embezzling.

I was alone now because the long arm of the law had caught up to him in Independence. Dad had given me all the money he had left to get me a start in Oregon. The money was gone now, and most of it went to the wagon master. The only thing I had to remind me of them was the knife. I was going over this body's memories in order to understand the *why* of this trip. At the age of thirteen and small, I had little chance of making it all the way there without help. Those people making the same trip had problems of their own and didn't need to take on more. My parents were taken away before any arrangements could be made.

It was still early in the day when I reached the small grove of trees. Most of them were not much taller than I was, but the undergrowth was pretty thick. There was a small pond being fed by an even smaller stream, and the water looked inviting. I scooped a handful to taste. It wasn't as cold as I hoped for but contained no bitterness. There were lots of tracks around to indicate some animals stopped to drink and a small fire pit from the two-legged ones.

I looked off to the south and could see the wagon train moving away. I felt nothing for it and wondered why. In fact, I had not had an emotional response to anything since I took over this body. I didn't remember if it was common for me, *The Nomadic Ghost*. I had no memory of who I was last time but knew it happened often—this moving from one body to the next. Each time I was required to do something for the spirits who called me. Each was different, and I had little or no memory of any of them. The job of those who called me was to keep a body alive until I finished what they wanted.

I felt the need to watch the wagons move off and then scan behind them for something. It wasn't long before I caught sight of a small band of Indians. I thought they must be following the wagons but noticed the direction was different. They were headed toward me instead. I saw six riders on horseback and one person walking or more like being dragged. I said to no one there, "I may be in big trouble here. They probably know about the water hole and could camp here or just drink and move on."

The need to stay out of sight was becoming obvious, as I had no idea how to handle six full-grown men or seven, counting the walker. I used the small trees for cover as I moved up the stream bed, looking for a place to hide. If the group was to camp here, they would need some firewood, and there wasn't much of it around. I couldn't stay near the creek, or they might see me while checking for something to burn. The prairie grass came up to the tree line and offered some cover if I managed to stay low enough.

I found an animal path going out from the bushes and followed it for a few yards. Deer or some other animals had bedded down just off the trail, and it gave me a place to lie down. The grasses didn't give me complete cover but maybe enough to keep from being seen. I kept my head up to watch and not expose myself.

When the Indians reached the pond area, they hobbled the horses and unloaded several bundles. I could hear the clink of bottles as they hollered for the woman they had been dragging along. I couldn't understand them but could see she was an Indian also and they needed her to prepare something to eat from one of the bags. They would be eating it cold as no one went looking for firewood. Maybe they already knew there wouldn't be any.

I hadn't noticed at first; a small person was in their company. I rose up a little more and saw a girl aged four or five with blond hair. She went to help the woman but didn't seem to know what was expected of her. One of the men swatted her across the head and pushed her away. She sat down and seemed to be crying until something was said.

I ducked back down and thought I should put the body to sleep as it needed rest more than anything. The sun was high overhead, and I had no cover from it, but sleep came and told me a story. I think you would call it a dream, except it must have been from my past. The grey uniform indicated a confederate soldier. I was sitting on a limb of a tree and holding a long-range musket. Smoke was still coming from the barrel when the fifty-caliber round from the other side hit my head. Whoever I shot must have been the target as I then left the body to end up here. The dream cycle ended, and no more information was allowed to pass through.

The men must have found some alcohol, as I slept with the sound of glass bottles breaking and much noisy celebrating. They drank themselves into a stupor and began to fall asleep as the sun was going down. I had slept long enough to give the body the needed rest it required, but now I would have to find something to eat. I couldn't shoot anything for fear of waking the six Indians, not that there was anything to shoot at. There had been enough noise to chase away any game interested in getting a drink.

I felt the urge to get a better look at the now unconscious group. I crawled in close and could see the woman had found a blanket, wrapped the girl up, and went to sleep. My body went into stealth mode as I got close to the first man. There was a red line about the width of my knife blade on his neck. I took it to mean I should insert my knife there. The quick jab put the blade up to the hilt and had it sticking out the other side. He jerked once, and then I watched as his spirit departed. It felt very familiar as I pulled the knife out and looked around.

I expected trouble, but no one moved. I saw the little red line on the next man's neck and slid over to him while trying to be as quiet as possible. The second one was the same as the first, and I moved into position for the third and fourth ones. I got the same results, but the fifth one started to gag and threw up on the last one in line, waking him up.

I pulled the big handgun out and waited a few seconds while the two made lots of noise. They barely settled down when the number five guy noticed me sitting just a foot or two from him. I cocked the hammer on the S&W and leveled it at him. He jumped up as it fell on the cartridge, and the bullet caught him a lot lower than I wanted. He fell on top of the sixth man, and they struggled to get up while I worked with both hands to get the hammer pulled back for another shot.

Number six was quicker than shit and had his rifle up while ratcheting a shell into the chamber. His aim would have been good, but the other Indian rolled into him and spoiled it. I did a better job of getting my shot to line up, and though the gun almost rolled me over, the bullet hit him in the left eye and took some brain tissue out the back of his skull.

The number five guy had retrieved a tomahawk and was about to hit me as I got the hammer back again and caught him a little higher on the body this time.

By then, I had an audience of two watching to see what would happen. They sat up but didn't move from their location. I expected the woman to react but knew she wasn't armed.

"Do you speak English?" I asked while replacing the three spent cartridges in the six-shooter.

"I do," said the little girl. She pointed at the woman. "She doesn't know how."

"How old are you?"

"I'll be five pretty soon." She had the look of not knowing when that would be.

"Do you know if there is any food here?"

She motioned to the woman and used her hand to indicate eating something.

There was no movement; the woman sat as if in a trance. The girl slapped her arm and said, "Wake up. He wants some food."

It was just enough to get her to recognize the fact I hadn't moved or threatened either her or the girl. She must have thought I possessed some magic to have killed the six braves. She rummaged around some packing and found a bit of jerky. She handed it to the girl and sat back down on her blanket.

The girl had no fear of me but didn't like getting close to the dead men. I got up and went to them and sat next to the woman. She then noticed how small I was; she was larger, both in height and weight. I found an empty bottle and asked the girl, "Can you rinse this out and fill it with water?"

She looked at me as if I had spoken a foreign language.

"Just put some water in it."

"I can do that."

I'll have to remember to keep it simple; I didn't think there would be enough alcohol left in it to matter. I washed down the jerky and thought there would be a lot of work to do here. I couldn't leave the dead men by the water, and the horses might be hard for me to handle. What should I do about the little girl? Did the woman understand what had happened, and would she cooperate?

It was still early into the night, but a big moon had made it bright enough to see everything. I took a closer look at the two and could see the woman had been treated badly. She had scars and fresh cuts on her face and both arms. They weren't deep but must have been used to keep control over her. I didn't understand enough about their social status and was just guessing. The little girl wore a ragged dress, and her hair was dirty and unkempt. More questions would have to wait till morning as I had things to do.

I motioned for the woman to follow me and went to look at the horses. They could not get to the water because of the hobble, so I indicated she should remove the rope holding the leg up on the one with the US ARMY brand on its rump. I held the rein and noticed that only one of the others had a saddle and bridle. They must have been taken in some raid, maybe the same one where they got the little girl. The woman removed the saddles and then checked all the animals for wear and tear.

We took the horses in turn to the pond and let them drink before hobbling them again. I removed the bridles and mouth rope from all of them so they could munch on the prairie grass without interference. The Indian woman was familiar with the process of hobbling and handling horses. It would have been hard for me to get even one to lift a leg for the hobble.

The little girl had gone back to sleep, and I indicated the woman should join her. Conversation was going to be minimal until we found some words in common. I then set about picking up the broken bottles and placing the glass in the fire pit. There was no wood to burn, but the pit looked like a safe place to put the shards. The next thing of interest was any and all weapons the dead men had accumulated. One of them had shot at me with a rifle, and I picked it up to get a look. It was a repeater of the same caliber as the pistol I had, which would make it easier to know what type of ammo would go with it. There was one more like it as I read the name *Henry .44*.

There were bows and arrows, but they were too hard-strung for me to use. Each Indian had a knife, and two had the hatchets they used as tomahawks. Several blankets held contraband from their last raid, and I went through those looking for anything that might be useful. They did manage to get a good supply of .44 cartridges, as one blanket held twelve boxes of twenty-five each. My math didn't go that high, so I left the count undone. Most of the other stuff looked like trading pieces, but one bundle had six pairs of boots. They were all too big for me to use, but four of them had handguns stuffed inside. They were all cap and ball pistols, and I couldn't find any powder or caps. There was a chunk of lead but no mold for it.

I knew from past experience that men seldom traveled at night, but I still held watch for several hours before letting the body sleep. It didn't occur to me that my past came up to tell me about the night travel thing. I kept watch as a ghost while the body got more rest.

Day Three

The sun came up early to start warming the air. I moved out into the open to get a feel for it. This small body didn't hold the heat, so the sun felt good on my back. The front half of me must have gotten too much sun yesterday, as the skin felt warm to the touch. The woman was up and getting something together in the form of food while the girl slept a little longer. We woke her up in time to eat some hard biscuits, jerky, and water. I knew the food thing would not work for long, as this body would need more protein, and I had six of them on the hoof, but only if we got desperate. The rifles were big enough to take down a buffalo, elk, or deer. I just hadn't seen any.

I guessed the six Indians had not been my target, or I would have jumped already. I needed some names or would just call them Indian and girl. "What's your name?" I asked the girl.

"I'm Patty," she said, "and her name is Ina."

Just then, Ina looked up to see why her name was called.

I looked at both of them and said, "Patty, Ina, I am John. Now, Patty, do you know your last name?"

She looked at me and shook her head. The last name would be important in tracking down her family. Without it, I might not even try. Besides, I was headed to Oregon, and I'm not sure where she came from or would have been going.

My trip to Oregon might not be necessary, or I might still be on the wagon train going there. I had to wonder what this set of ghosts wanted me to do. Killing Indians might be part of it, or they just might have gotten in the way. It looked as if they supplied me with transportation and companions. Now what to do with those companions?

Getting rid of the bodies was more important now. I used the halter ropes to bind together the feet of all six dead men.

"Ina, put a saddle on the army horse and take the hobble off," I said.

She must have understood my need for a horse and did exactly as I had asked. I looked around but couldn't see any place to drop the bodies into. So covering them up might not work. I didn't care one way or the other but didn't know how Ina would take it.

I put the bridle on, climbed into the saddle, and motioned for Ina to adjust the stirrups. The setting for this saddle barely let my feet reach them with the last adjustment hole. I guess it would have to do, as both saddles seemed to be the same. I started to pull the dead guys when Ina waved for me to stop. "What's wrong?" I asked.

One of them had on an army jacket. She took it off, then waved me to go ahead. She held the coat to herself as if it meant something. I pulled the rope tight and headed east. The wind would normally come out of the west, so any scent from the dead men might not interfere with someone stopping for a drink. I suspected the night critters would raid the bodies for what was edible.

I found a buffalo wallow about a mile or so out and dumped the bodies in it after removing the ropes which tied them together. I didn't think the buffalo would like it much, but that would be their problem.

When I got back, Ina had cleaned up much of the mess and had packed most of the gear in the blankets. She had the saddle on the other horse and was waiting for instructions on what to do next. I had heard talk of a river west of here where the wagons might have trouble crossing. We put the halter ropes on the four Indian ponies and removed their hobbles. We tied them together, and Ina helped get Patty up on the Army horse with me.

"Hang on tight, sweetheart. We're going for a ride," I said.

I pointed to the west as Ina took the rope from the lead pony and fell in behind me as I started out. We walked the horses as straight as I could guess with the sun behind us. I could see some brown dots off in the distance and turned a little northerly to see if they might be a food source. An hour or two of easy walking brought us into range of a small buffalo herd. They had seen us coming but failed to recognize the danger to them. We stopped and dismounted, and I indicated to Ina to give me one of the rifles. I checked it for rounds and motioned she should wait here while I walked Army, the horse, up toward the herd. I used the horse to block a view of me until I was in range. I hadn't fired the rifle yet, and it seemed to be a natural fit except for the size. I tied the rein around my left arm and used it to support the gun while aiming it at one of the smaller animals. I sat on the ground and propped my elbow on my knee to keep the barrel trained on my target.

The kick from the gun and the jerk from the horse tried to send me in two different directions, but the aim had been good. Ina had put Patty on her horse and walked all five of them down toward the dead buffalo before I could get up. I'd have to find a better way to use the gun. With the rifle stock against my shoulder, I could barely reach the trigger.

Ina had started to butcher the kill before I got there and handed me the heart. I looked at her for advice and said, "What do I do with it?"

She indicated I should eat it.

I took my knife and cut the heart in half, and cut one half again. I then gave Ina and Patty each a quarter of the meat. "That's your share for helping in the hunt," I told them while I ate the other piece.

Ina was surprised I would be so generous and waited until Patty started to eat her share. On the other hand, I didn't know what the common practice would be for her tribe, but she would have to live by my rules. She had already conceded the leadership role to me.

It took all day to get the animal cut up and wrapped in the hide. Ina had cut a blanket for some of the meat and tied each piece up with strips cut from the same blanket. The next thing would be to locate a source of wood to cook and dry most of the meat. It had been a long day for all of us, and we slept on the prairie.

Day Four

In the morning, we started to pack everything on the horses. They weren't very enthusiastic about carrying the meat, but we didn't give them an option. We left enough of the buffalo parts to keep the prairie predators busy for a day or two. Then it was "Westward Ho!" as we went looking for the river and some trees for wood. It was getting late in the day when it looked like a darker area up ahead. We reached the river and could see trees on the other side, but the bank on this side was steep, and the river was a little rough at this point. I turned us north and followed the river upstream for a mile or two, where we could get down to the water and possibly cross. It was a lot calmer here.

I took the bag with the bullets in it and hung it over my back to keep the rounds dry. We coaxed the horses into the water and started across. The current was strong enough to prevent us from going straight, but the horses could see the other side and swam hard to get there. At about halfway, the horses could touch bottom, and we managed to get out without any real trouble. The west side of the river was lower and held some dead trees washed down during the spring run-off.

We unloaded the horses, hobbled them, and then hung the meat in one of the trees to keep from losing any to the wildlife. Ina started clearing a place for a fire while I gathered up some smaller branches to get one going and handed her my flint. She used the backdrop of the biggest log. Then she removed the grass with a hatchet, saving some to start the fire with. Patty wanted to help, so Ina showed her how to weave the grass together to make a torch. I wasn't sure what

13

she would use for grease, but maybe there was enough of it in the buffalo meat.

Riding instead of walking had allowed me to regain some of the strength I had lost, and I used it to chop up a few bigger branches for the fire. We would do more in the morning while getting the meat ready to cook. Our food had been limited to hard biscuits and jerky so far, but now we could get some real meat. However, it would have to wait till morning.

Sleep came quickly but didn't last long. Some marauding creatures made the horses nervous, and I fired a couple of rounds from the handgun to keep them at bay. I reached out with the spirit, and it scared them more than the noise did. I had to experiment with what I could and couldn't do without killing the body.

Days Five & Six

Morning came and caught me tending the fire. Ina had banked it up against the big log, and I just added some fuel to it. The short night was for me, *The Nomadic Ghost*, while the body managed to get plenty of rest.

"Ina, what do we need to cook some of this meat?" I indicated the fire and meat.

She drew a couple of things in the loose dirt that looked like a fork and straight sticks. I gestured for length. She took my hand and held it out, then measured from shoulder to fingertips. Then she held up two fingers. Next, she pulled my arms out and indicated from hand to hand.

I got the message and went off with one of the axes to cut three tree limbs. Two of them would be forked and the other straight. I recognized the design of a spit to cook one or more roasts on. It would have to be green wood to keep from burning and big enough to accommodate more than one chunk of buffalo.

Ina took the horses down to the river for a drink then roped them together loosely so they could forage on the river grasses. By the time I got back, she had set up a three-sided box for the fire pit and was slicing strips off one of the buffalo chunks. I had no idea what would be roasts or steaks or something else. She had done this before, and I never had—as far as I knew. The strips were placed on the inside of the three logs so they would be facing the fire and would dry out.

"What can I do to help?" I asked.

She indicated I should strip the bark off the sticks before she

15

could use them.

The forked sticks then went into the ground on the outside of the side logs. Two of the meat chunks went on the straight piece I brought and then placed over the fire. The two buffalo roasts were unevenly placed, so one hung lower than the other, depending on which one was closest to the fire. They could be rotated, so they cooked one side a little faster. We would have to turn the spit halfway around to cook the meat on both sides.

We spent the two days cutting and cooking buffalo meat and eating as we went. The dried strips turned into jerky; the roasts were charred on the outside to keep them from spoiling.

I had left it up to Ina and hoped she knew what to do with them. I was a raw recruit when it came to preserving food. I only knew the weather and temperature could cause some problems. Ina had kept Patty busy enough to stay out of trouble, and she was willing to help wherever possible.

Day Seven

The next day we started to get things together, as I wanted to get down to the trail and see if I could hook up with the next wagon train coming through. I had no idea what would happen to Ina and Patty but guessed one would be accepted and the other might not. Blond hair and blue eyes would be an attraction to most of the travelers, but an Indian woman could be a problem to deal with. Then there was this body I had which was rejected on the wagon train it came from.

Ina hobbled the horses so we could load the supplies without the trouble of fighting each one as we loaded it. We saddled the two horses that had shoes and got the bundles ready to load when a shot rang out. Someone was shooting at us, and I hit the deck before they fired another round. I had gotten in behind the big log we used as a backdrop for the fire and could see several Indians on top of the bluff directly across from us. I hadn't recognized the itch in the back of my head while busy with the horses.

They pushed their ponies over the edge and into the river without firing another round. We hadn't crossed there because of the height of the riverbank on that side. Now I saw eight of them—all on horseback—hit the water with a big splash each. I retrieved one of the rifles and a box of shells and sat down on the other side of the log I had just hidden behind. The Indians wouldn't be able to shoot at me while trying to get the horses lined up toward us. The current wanted them to go downstream even though the water looked calm on the surface.

I took the rifle and waited till all the Indians were struggling with their horses and shot the last one. I couldn't hold the gun in the normal position, so I placed the butt of the stock against the big log and let it take the recoil for me. The front end of the gun jumped up a bit, but the bullet had already left the barrel. Dead Eye Johnny had taken one out with seven more to go. I smiled at the thought of how dumb it was.

"Tamp down on the emotions and get on with the slaughter." No one was listening to me as I talked my way through the next shots. "I can see the lead Indian isn't paying attention yet, so let's just work from back to front until they catch on."

My marksmanship had always been good, as a fond memory of past lives flittered through my current brain, but the smell of gunpowder and sparking of flint indicated a different time. Now I had a better handle on the recoil and said, "Thanks for the help, guys. Is this the thing you brought me here to do?" I asked the spirits who had called me to this mission.

I didn't get an answer, but the six remaining Indians were now paying more attention and trying to shield themselves with the neck and head of the horse they were on. I hated the thought of killing the horses, but I had to get them turned downstream before they could get to the lower—but level—area in the river. I was about to fire the next round when a shot rang out just off to my right. "Ina, what are you doing?" I asked as one more brave slipped away from his pony, leaving five to be targeted.

"Shoot them; they hurt Ina." It was the first words she had spoken in English.

The gunfire should make the rest think about going down the river instead of crossing here.

The horses they had were now confused and tried to turn back to the other side and, in doing so, exposed the riders for a few seconds.

Both Ina and I fired then, and two more of the Indians separated from the horses they had been on. Now the horses were starting to panic as their riders kept trying to use them as shields. With three left, I picked out the one furthest from us and shot the horse through the neck. The bullet hit the Indian in the head as he was trying to see who was doing the shooting. Ina had fired several more shots without hitting either the men or the horses. The remaining two made it to the rapids before getting out of sight.

I jumped up and motioned Ina to follow me as we ran downriver to see if we could get another shot before they could get out of the water. The rapids area went on for a while, and when we could see the horses, there was no one with them.

The itch in the back of my head indicated a problem, so I shifted to ghost mode and separated enough to blur the image. Just then, one of the two remaining men jumped out of the reeds with a tomahawk, but the illusion slowed him for a second, and Ina put a bullet through his abdomen. I shifted back and pulled the trigger, sending a slug into his chest. The last one made it to the other bank, and both Ina and I shot at him. He slid back down the slope and into the river. If my math was correct, then that would be all of them. We watched several bodies float away.

"Thanks, Ina; good shooting."

She started to say something but couldn't find the right words. I said, "It's okay now. Let's get back to camp and make sure everything is still in order."

Patty was holding the lead ropes on four ponies. "I have horses," she said. Four of the Indian ponies made it out of the water.

"Patty, that's very good. I think you can keep those if you want to. Ina and I are going to load the other horses and get moving. There should be a wagon train on the trail soon, and we need to be stationed where we can meet them." I thought Patty might be able to trade the animals for a new family.

Ina might be looked at differently when we meet up with the pilgrims moving west. I'm not sure what I needed to do yet either. I had no indication of success, as I was still here.

I thought the Indians must have followed us after finding the dead ones and had no reason to think differently. Three horses were missing and probably downriver somewhere. Also, there was no guarantee that all eight Indians were dead, but I felt as if their spirits departed after each one was hit.

We were going to have a problem with the growing number of horses, and I said, "How are we going to keep control of them?"

There were now ten of them—four backpacked and two riding with saddles. Patty's horses would have to be tied to one of ours with the hope they would not try to go on their own someplace. While I was mulling this over, Ina started tying the new horses to each other's tails and then to the tail from her horse. I wouldn't have thought of such a thing, but as we started out, each one followed. I wondered if it was an Indian trick.

As Patty, the horses, and I were not used to traveling in this fashion, we had to make several stops. Since we didn't have to hurry, we found two more ponies that had made it out of the water. We now had twelve. I had no idea what we could do with them. The horses from the Indians could be ridden, but would they take a saddle? We already had two riding horses and only two saddles, so it was a moot question at this time.

When we stopped for the night, we made no plans to make a fire as we were now on the open prairie. There were some bushes along the river, but tree stumps indicated their removal. "I think we must be close to the trail, as someone had cut those trees for firewood or repair work."

Ina nodded in agreement as if she knew what I said. Maybe she was around the white man enough to understand the meaning of some words. As of now, she wasn't talking.

Food and chores were done in a reasonable fashion but time-consuming. Taking care of twelve horses and three people meant we would have to stop earlier, as it was well past dark when we finally hit the hay. There would be no sleeping in either, and I made myself a promise to never take up farming. This time of year, the sun comes up early and goes down late, making for a short night of sleep.

Day Eight

Like I said, the sun comes up early. Fortunately, this body got enough rest as I played sentry for the duration of the night. We woke to the sound of gunfire, but this time it was much further away. The stillness of the prairie let it carry for some distance. "Now who's doing the shooting"? I asked.

We didn't seem to be in immediate danger, as I was missing the little tweaking in the back of my head. The horses were nervous but not trying to get away while Patty ran to check on her new possessions. I hollered, "Don't let them step on you. Watch your feet!" A horse could break the bones in her feet the way they were prancing around. Ina went to help her as they tried to settle the herd down. They weren't going to run off, as they were all hobbled.

The gunfire continued and even escalated, but some of it seemed further away than others. My instincts told me several different guns were being used. The big muskets had a very heavy sound, while some of the pistols had more of a pop. Then there was the sound from the repeating rifles.

"Ina, saddle Army for me, and I'll ride down that way to see if we will be getting into any danger today."

She complied and said, "Take gun." It was only the second time she spoke in English.

Riding and carrying the rifle would be more of a problem than a help, so I opted for the handgun and checked to make sure it was fully loaded.

I was constantly reminded of the possibility of trouble by the little itch in the back of my head. It didn't seem to indicate much more than being very cautious. We had come closer to the trail than I thought, as it only took a few minutes to reach the area where the wagon wheel ruts could be seen. There was no cover on either side of the river, but the distance across gave me some protection from being shot at or at least hit. The horse might be targeted first, so I kept back from the river to prevent it from happening.

At this point in the migration route, the prairie is flat for many miles, and I could see across the river from some distance. The wagon train was backed up against the river and using it for a backdrop. The Indians were making passes across the other side of the wagons and firing the same kind of rifles I had taken from the ones I killed a couple of nights back. The return fire from the camp was more or less handguns and percussion cap rifles. It dawned on me the eight Indians I intercepted upriver had intended to guard this side of the river and take some shots from here. No one in the wagon train had noticed me, and the Indians were too busy to look my way. In fact, the Indians could have planned on sneaking across the river here, as it was the calmest location I had seen so far.

I watched as four more Indians worked their way upriver along the bank in an attempt to get behind the pioneers. The water wasn't very deep there, but they had to get into it as the bank was undercut by the spring runoff. They were holding rifles very similar to the Henry .44s I had come to possess. My first thought was someone must have sold or traded with the Indians for them to have so many of the same make weapon.

I was trying to think of some way to warn the travelers when Ina rode up. She left Patty in charge of the Indian ponies and brought both rifles and the bag of bullets with her.

"What did you do with the horses?"

"Hobbled," she said.

The Indians in the river could see us but assumed one boy and one woman couldn't stop them from getting to the wagon train.

Ina wanted to start shooting as soon as she got off her horse. I put a halt to it as I dismounted and took the second rifle from her. "Wait till they get out of the water."

I guessed the wagoners would like to have the rifles and any ammunition the Indians had with them. We ground-tied the horses, walked down to the river, and sat to watch. Ina took her cue from me and sat down. We checked both rifles to make sure they were fully loaded and waited for the Indians to reach the ramp where previous trains had crossed.

We were nothing more than a curiosity to the four as they gathered at the foot of the ramp. I hand signaled for Ina to take the first shot, and I would follow hers. Firing one at a time would let us keep from shooting the same target and wasting our ammunition. I pushed the butt of my gun into the dirt to help with the recoil.

The Indians had started up the ramp and ignored us until Ina fired her gun. She missed, but I made sure mine counted, and we were down to three. Her next shot was better, but now the Indians were moving to get in position to shoot back. Only two had the opportunity. I reduced that to one as the last one returned fire, but he was in such a hurry he missed badly.

The shooting attracted the attention of someone in the camp, and the last Indian failed to notice at his expense. The pistol fire stopped him from getting another shot off and left all four above the waterline. Their rifles and ammunition now belonged to the travelers. I waved for someone to retrieve the weapons.

Ina left to make sure Patty wasn't having any problems with the horses. I waited until the pioneer had gathered up the guns and ammo and took them up to the camp. I mounted up on Army and road south along the river to see if any more attackers would try to infiltrate via the river route.

The wagon train gunmen now had better rifles and were doing a better job of taking the Indians and their ponies out. The shooting stopped as I returned to the ramp area on my side and exchanged waves with several members of the troupe. It appeared as if the Indians had retreated for now, and it gave the travelers time to clean up the mess and tend to the wounded.

I waited as a rider from the camp came down to the river and started across. He had two things on his mind, and the first was to determine if the water was low enough to get the wagons across. He didn't have any trouble crossing and proceeded to his second reason.

"Hello. Thank you for the assistance," he said. When his horse came up out of the water, he got a better look at me. "John Vanderwick! What the hell are you doing here?"

I didn't know his name but recognized him as the person who supplied me with a handgun and some shells. "I thought it was my job to rescue you and the rest of the camp. I've made good use of the handgun you loaned me. By the way, I never got your name before I left."

"Oh, sorry, it's Tom Brown, and it is good to see you again. I had dreadful dreams of seeing you starve to death or shoot yourself."

I turned to look back up the river and could see Ina and Patty were on their way with the herd of horses. "Well, Tom Brown, the rest of my contingent is about to arrive."

"They belong to you?"

"In a sense, they do, but they aren't as much property as they are companions."

"How did you come to have so many horses?"

"Dumb luck, I guess. Are you planning to cross the river today?"

"We were held up by the Indians, or we would have been out of here by now. We're running behind schedule and will try to cross if the Indians don't attack again. The wagon master will make the decision."

Ina and Patty arrived, and I introduced them to Tom. "This is Ina, and I have no idea what tribe she might be from. The little girl is Patty, and I think she lost her parents someplace. Both of them were being held by some Indians, and I managed to separate them. How did your group fare against the attackers?"

"We have some wounded and lost four adults and two kids. The two boys who used to tease you wanted to show how tough they were and went outside the line of wagons."

"Well, I hope the wounded recover. I don't see the need for my group to cross, so we'll wait here for you."

"Thanks again for the help," he said and turned his horse back to the river.

I watched as he worked his horse up and down the deepest part. I was guessing he needed to measure for the best location the wagons would need. If it was too deep, they might lose any wagon that couldn't touch bottom. I thought the Conestogas might be a problem, but it was beyond my scope of things to worry about, so I let it go.

John Vanderwick had been getting a formal education back in Rhode Island but lacked any knowledge of frontier life. It was part of the reason he wasn't accepted by the members of the wagon train. That would change now, but there would be other problems to work through.

The day dragged on, and it looked as if the wagon train would wait till tomorrow before they tried to ford the river. There was a lot of movement, but no attempt to come down the ramp was made except for the Indian women retrieving the four men we shot. Some kind of peace must have been brokered to let them through.

I took the horses, two at a time, to the river and let them drink their fill. Patty wanted to take hers, so I made her take them one at a time. Even for me, the two horses tended to separate and pull me in different directions. The horses I held tried to back away from the river as the two remaining horses from the Indians came floating by. They must have been caught on something to take this long to get here. I dropped the ropes of the two I had and jumped into the river. One of the horses was still trying to keep its head above water and not doing very well. I knew the other one was dead, so I swam to the surviving one and got hold of his mouth rope. I turned him toward shore and tried to pull him, but the current was trying to take us downstream. Ina jumped in and helped get us going in the right direction, and we managed to get it to solid ground. This one wasn't thirsty anymore.

I had run out of fingers trying to count the number of horses we had and hoped it wasn't a bad omen. Our latest acquisition could barely stand, let alone move, so we left him there while taking care of the rest of the horses. When he found the strength, he joined the others. We didn't bother hobbling him. It might take a day or more for him to fully recover.

The horses munched on prairie grass while we ate dried buffalo meat and the last of the hard biscuits. It would be daylight for a few more hours, so we sat and watched to see what might happen.

Tom Brown came down the ramp, crossed the river to our side, and dismounted. "John, we have a stalemate going over there, and the chief wants to talk to the wizard. I'm sure that's not the right word for it, but he lost many men to someone outside the wagon train. He couldn't count them with both hands. Do you know what he might want?"

I thought it over for a minute. "Maybe," I answered. "That's where all the ponies came from. He might listen to Ina and me, but I'm not going over there and leave the horses and Patty here."

"I can fill in for you till you get back, but I'd sure like to hear the conversation."

"I'm guessing the chief wants a private talk, so no one from the wagon train can go with us."

"If it works out, I don't think anyone will care, but you might not want to take Ina with you."

"Why is that?"

"She has the signs of a used woman."

"You're talking about the scars and cut marks on her face and arms?"

"Yeah, the tribes mark loose women that way."

"Well, either he sees me with her or not at all."

"You have a much stronger will than I gave you credit for."

"I think it would be lack of fear now. Being close to death allows one to have the freedom to assert oneself."

I looked at Ina and asked, "Do you understand what we were talking about?"

She nodded her head.

"Patty," I said, "Ina and I are going across the river. I want you to stay and take care of the horses. Tom will help you if you need him."

"I can do that."

Tom asked, "Are you going to take those rifles with you?"

"I think they might help make the point we will need to get the chief to understand the problem he has."

With that, Ina and I rode our horses into the river, and Tom wished us luck.

The ride through the wagon train was interesting but not worth worrying about. Most of the travelers recognized me and failed to do more than point. On the other hand, maybe they were pointing at Ina instead. Some of the men were digging holes I assumed would hold the dead members of this troupe. I looked straight ahead and avoided any option for eye contact.

The Indians were about a quarter of a mile out and waiting to see who would be coming to talk to them. Their women were still moving the dead to a location where they had a wagon. I could see at least ten bodies and several horses just past the perimeter of the camp.

I stopped at about the halfway point and waited to see who the chief would send to greet us. Ina was most impressive as she sat straight up and rested the butt of her rifle on her right thigh with the barrel aimed at the sky. I held mine across the saddle, making sure it didn't point at anyone. One young brave rode in to have a look. He came past us and circled back. When he spit on Ina, she shot him. Fortunately, it wasn't a killing shot, and he rode back before falling off his horse. He might die in a day or two unless someone treats his wound. There was no reaction from any member of the tribe.

I sat still and waited for a better invitation to arrive. It came after some conversation when the chief and one of their women came to talk. The woman was not on horseback and appeared to be less than willing to come along.

Ina got down off her horse to indicate subservience to me. She held her rifle as if she would shoot anyone treating either of us badly. I hadn't expected Ina to take to her role so easily and so quickly. She must have thought if I could kill Indians without showing any emotion, then she could at least defend me at all costs. I had given her something she probably never had, and now it was payback time for anyone getting in her way.

The chief was carrying a rifle like the one I had and made a point of holding it up for me to look at. I rode up beside him and let him get a good look at mine. He said something to the woman.

She spoke in haltering English. "You get this from brave?"

Ina answered in her tongue and must have told the other woman to repeat in English.

"She does not speak English and says you have killed many braves."

"This is true."

There was some more conversation with the chief.

"Chief asks to see your feet."

"Why?"

"To match the size of prints at water hole."

I put one foot on his horse, so he could get a look at it. Then he pointed to the woman, and she looked to see if it was the same one. She nodded her head as if to say yes. Then more conversation was used.

"Chief wants to know how many braves you kill."

I was going to take the whole amount and not let Ina be considered for the ones she shot. I held up two hands to indicate six and said, "Six in the first group at the water hole." Then held up both hands again for a count of eight and said, "Eight in the second group crossing the river." Then held up one hand with four fingers and said, "Four in the last group behind the wagons."

There was a lot of jabbering between the chief and the woman, but they knew Ina understood their language and had problems speaking mine. Ina interrupted them to say something, and the woman said, "She wants the chief to know you didn't kill them all by yourself and she helped you by shooting three in the second group and one in the third group."

"That is correct, but we acted as one."

When she reported to the chief, it seemed to make Ina very pleased.

The chief, on the other hand, didn't seem so happy. He knew one word of English and said, "How?"

I gave him the show by pulling the ghostly part of me out far enough to look like a shadow sitting next to the body.

The woman dropped to the ground and hid her head in her arms while the chief said something very excitedly.

"It is a spirit man/boy, and we are in his presence," the woman said without looking up.

Ina reached for her and brought her to her feet. "Up," she said, along with some stuff I didn't understand.

"She said you have great power and have saved her from being hurt. You have shared a buffalo heart with her and made her like an even to you."

"She does what I ask of her, but I do not make her do anything she would object to. We work together as one." Apparently, some of what I am rubbed off on Ina, and she is showing off to the chief.

There was more conversation between the woman and the chief.

"Chief wants to know how many in the camp are dead."

"The total is six, four men and two boys." I wasn't going to ask how many braves he lost. It had to be well over twenty, and their ability to keep fighting was greatly diminished.

It was worse than I thought, as Ina questioned them while I was getting a lesson in their language. The spirit I am has used multiple forms of speech over the centuries. With each converted conversation, I was able to gather more understanding of what was being said.

The chief said, "We got the guns when we raided a trader wagon, but there are few bullets left. There is no way to find more, and the guns will be useless. Our braves do not know how to use them as well as the white man does. We thought the rifles would take care of everything and abandoned our arrow and stealth."

Ina asked, "What will you do?"

He responded, "The guns do not kill the white man, but they kill my people. We will throw away the rifles and go back to our old ways."

There was some more talk between the woman and the chief. I was able to pick up most of it by now. I kept quiet and let them think they had to deal with Ina. It was good for Ina and hard for the chief, but it worked in my favor and also helped the woman gain some prestige with her tribe.

The Indian woman, still talking in her tongue, asked, "How much needed to be told?"

The chief said, "Tell him all of it."

I let her repeat most of it.

When she finished, I said, "I know how many men the tribe has lost. Now you need to tell the chief I will not kill more of his party. You have lost enough men. He may leave the guns with no bullets here. I will take the wagon train west to Oregon, and he will not see me again."

She relayed my offer to the chief, who said, "This is the most powerful of the white man. We will do as you ask."

I nodded my head to the chief, and he did the same to me. He turned his horse and rode back to the raiding party. The woman bowed low to me and followed the chief. Ina mounted her horse, and we sat until the Indians tossed down the rifles and left the area. Those in the camp saw what happened, and some ran out to gather up the rifles.

Ina and I rode back through the camp and across the river to check on Patty and the horses. Tom was anxious to hear from us. "Okay, what happened?"

"The chief was willing to leave and dropped the rifles also. They were out of ammunition."

"We were close to out also. I think we can get more at Fort Henry before we get into the mountains."

I wondered if they named the fort after the guy who made the rifles.

Ina was glad to be back, and Patty was thrilled to see her, as they hugged as soon as Ina got off her horse. I lacked the emotion for it but knew it was a good thing.

Tom said, "It's probably too late to move the wagons, so I expect the boss to get an early start in the morning. Did you have any conversation with him?"

"No, I didn't. He might think I'm holding a grudge for the way I was treated and the fact that he took all my money and supplied me with so little help. I think he owes me something, and you can tell him when you see him."

"I know what you mean. He seems to be a bit self-centered but does know the business and was able to keep the Indians at bay. I'll tell him what you said. I'd like to sit down and talk to you about what went on with the Indians, but I best get over there now and see what can be done to get us moving in the morning."

It was close to the end of the day, and we made sure the horses had their fill of water. The last horse had recovered enough that it was easy to move. We didn't bother hobbling it but made sure the rest were as we settled in for the night.

I let the body rest while keeping a ghostly lookout for anything out of the ordinary. This body was gradually adjusting to the lifestyle, but it still hurt to sleep on the ground. I managed to shut off the pain and would deal with it in the morning.

Day Nine

Noise from the movement of animals and wagons and other sounds of a camp being taken apart woke us. We had our horses off to one side so as not to hinder the wagons when they emerged from the water. Tom Brown was the first one coming over, and he trailed a rope which was anchored on the far bank. It marked the river where he found the water was lowest as a guide for the pioneers as they started across.

The prairie schooners, with their high wheels, were lined up first. The Conestogas would be last, as they might need help to keep them from being washed downstream. Tom set an anchor and tied the rope to it, then rode back across to get the first wagon going. He took the upriver side to keep the mules and wagons from pushing him downstream and led the four mules into the water. Each wagon had another rider guiding the animals into and across the river.

When the first one made it without any problems, Tom went back for another one. It was an all-day process, and the women set up a cookstove and started the stew pot. I offered the buffalo meat, and they added in some after cutting it into small pieces. Ina wasn't happy about giving up our meat, but now she didn't have to cook it or carry it. What meat was left over went into a small barrel with lots of salt.

The prairie schooners pulled into a big circle, and the teams were unharnessed and allowed to graze on the wildflowers and grasses. It was now time to get the Conestogas into and out of the river. All the trail hands were on board for this, as the water would make the wagons float a little in the deepest part of the river. The oxen were shorter-legged and would have some problems also as four men took lead ropes for them and started across.

This must have been done many times in the past, and the boss knew his stuff. The second Conestoga waited till the first one was out of the water, and then they started. The riders were familiar with the effort while working the oxen through the deep part and on to the shore.

Okay, we took care of the Indian problem, and now the wagon train had crossed the river, and I'm still here. So what am I waiting for?

The wagon boss came over to me and said, "I'm told you need an apology from me, and I sincerely give it to you. We have lost several days because of the trouble with the Indians. Thank you for getting them to agree to leave us alone. I have some questions, as do most of the people in our troupe. You left us while looking as if you couldn't last one more day. It's my fault, but I would like to know how you managed to survive. Also, you have a collection of horses and a couple of, ah, people with you. Who are they, and where did they come from?"

"First, you took some gold coins from me, and I would like them back. You didn't fulfill your end of the bargain. My survival came from the mother of necessity. Next, the people with me and the horses were in the possession of members from the same tribe of Indians you encountered. They didn't give them up willingly. The chief attacking your group was much moved by the fact I eliminated more of his men than you did. They ran out of bullets and would have gone to flaming arrows for the next attack. I don't know if he intends to attack other wagon trains, as I didn't require that of him."

"Okay, before I ask about the horses, tell me why the woman with you shot the Indian before you talked to the chief."

"Yeah, he was just asked to check us out, and when he spit on her, she shot him. I think everyone saw."

"She has the marks of a dirty woman, and the tribes would never let her forget it."

"Sometimes people get into situations they have no control over. I have not accused her of anything and have let her join me in getting revenge on the tribe that marked her. She will be treated nicely by you and the people here, or she will take revenge on them."

"Wow, that's asking a lot."

32

"I don't think so. Most of these people just want to get a new start in a better place. It's all she wants now. I think you and the men you hired may have a different outlook than the pioneers do."

"Yeah, you're right. Now tell me about the little girl."

"I have no idea where she came from or who her parents are or were. She was in the possession of the same group of Indians the woman was. I have to guess her parents died in a raid and they took the girl then. She doesn't know her last name."

"How many Indians were holding them?"

"When I encountered the group, there were six braves."

"Many of the group will ask you the same questions or ones that might affect them. You can refer them to me or answer them yourself."

"I'll do the best I can to keep from letting it bother me."

"I'm guessing the horses came from the Indians you managed to send to the happy hunting grounds."

"I don't know anything about hunting grounds, but yes, the horses came from the Indians I was able to remove from this existence. Two of the horses have shoes and saddles, but the rest are Indian ponies and might need to be trained before taking a saddle. Patty, the little girl, owns four horses, as she rescued them from the river. Ina, the woman, owns the other saddle horse, and I have taken possession of the one called Army."

"What about the rest of the horses?"

"They can be traded for but do not have shoes or saddles."

"You're not trying to sell them?"

"The gold you owe me is the only item of currency I want. The trade value of the horses can bring food or other types of usable items. We have some trade goods also for those who might be interested."

"We will be camped here for the rest of the day and get an early start in the morning. I will return your gold coins to you before we settle down for the night. I'll also make the announcement about the horses."

Ina and Patty had been listening but not interrupting. Patty said, "Do I have to give someone my horses?"

I looked at her and smiled. "You own those four horses and can do whatever you want with them. No one will take them from you without you telling them it's okay."

I thought I might have to take a shoe off to count the number of horses we could barter with, but my math got better when I eliminated Patty's four. Now take away mine and Ina's, and it leaves seven horses.

"Ina, do you want to get the boots and handguns out and whatever else we have in those blankets we can trade?"

I hadn't gone through all the stuff, as it seemed it was mostly clothing and bedding items. I wondered why the Indians kept the women's dresses and undergarments. She pulled out the men's boots and the cap and ball pistols along with the chunk of lead. One of the blankets had trading items meant to go to the Indians, I think.

We set everything out and waited to see who would be the first ones to get a look at our wares. It wasn't long before Tom came and brought a couple of outriders. "I hear you have some horses for sale."

"I think that might not be accurate. We can't use the money and are hoping to trade for things we can use."

Ina and Patty had separated our horses and left just the seven ponies. "We have seven Indian ponies up for trade. They may need to be broken in for a saddle/bridle setup, and they don't have shoes. Maybe you can get them shod at Fort Henry."

Some of the outriders had paid to go one way with the wagon train, and having a second horse would make it easier with a chance to sell or trade one at the end of the trip.

Ina asked, "Bullets?" as she pointed out the boxes of .44s we had.

"Set out five boxes for now," I said as I held up one hand's worth. "Some of the riders and pioneers may have use for them, but we can wait for now." We both knew the rifles dropped by the Indians were now in the hands of people in this group, but they probably didn't have ammunition for them. Some supplies could be had at Fort Henry, but if the need arose before we got there, then the bullets would be worth more in trade.

I walked with Tom and the outriders to where the seven horses were and said, "We separated the six horses we intend to keep. These seven have worked as pack animals and have been ridden by Indians, but none have been saddle broke or had a metal bit in their mouth. They haven't tried to run away, but we hobbled them every night anyway."

Tom took a quick look and said, "You have four mares and three stallions. The mares could be used for breeding, but I can't tell if any are pregnant at this time."

"I hadn't thought of it, but I can check for you and find out."

"What are you, a vet?"

"No, I just have a good sense of how they may want to brag." I put my head against the neck of the first mare as if to listen, then went on to each of the other three. What Tom and the others couldn't see is that I moved as a spirit inside each one enough to get a reading.

"Well, if you're interested in one already carrying, then you might pick the second one here. The others are not yet pregnant."

"How did you do that?"

"I think it's called talking. I asked, and they let me know. That one couldn't tell me when she was due."

"She doesn't look ready yet, so it could be a while—enough to get to Oregon, maybe. As riders, we don't have much to trade, so maybe we can work something else out."

"Well, let's get some of the pioneers here to see if they have an interest. If no one wants them, then we might do some talking. I can use a couple as pack animals, but I would still say five have to go."

"I can't see them adding problems to their already stretched workload. You might just be stuck with all those horses."

I could see he wanted one and was afraid they would all be gone before we finished the day. Just then, the cooks called for dinner, and we dropped everything and joined the rush to get some food. Ina and I waited for the rest to get their share, but Patty pushed her way past the adults and got a full plate. She hadn't had a good meal in some time and wasn't waiting in case they ran out. Several little girls saw what she did and joined in the me-first move. When I didn't stop Patty, the parents of the others didn't try to stop their kids. There was enough for everyone, and some left over for seconds anyway.

We finished eating and found several of the travelers looking over our trade goods. The bullets, boots, handguns, and lead were the things they were most interested in. The girls came over with Patty, and she showed them her horses. They had seen horses before and were more interested in the trinkets. There were beads and mirrors and knickknacks of various kinds. No one wanted the Indian ponies, even though several of the men looked at them.

Wagon trains are not the best places to do trading, as the pioneers generally take the things they need most and leave little room for anything else. The horses would bring a good price up in Oregon, but they were hard to keep as extras on the trip.

We traded the bullets for salt and jerky and got a canteen for a pair of boots. The ladies looked the clothing over and offered to make something for Ina and me to wear in exchange. I let them have all of it; they could fight each other for what they wanted. The handguns and lead were items in need, and we got a small saddle and bridle for Patty for them. I got my saddle adjusted so my feet fit the stirrups.

Tom came around late to see if the horses were still there. "What are you going to do with them?"

"We'll take them up to Fort Henry and see what they're worth."

"I sure could use one. I'd take that pregnant filly off your hands tonight, and you won't have to worry about her dropping the foal."

"You can't take care of any more than the one you're riding until we get to Oregon. If I gave her to you, I'd still have to watch her."

"Yeah, I'm sure you're right, but I would like to have her."

"We'll see. Maybe we can ride with you and get some help with all the horses till we get to the fort."

"I have to get an early start in the morning. I'll be riding out ahead of the wagons to make sure the route is clear and no one is sitting in wait."

"What would you do with the filly and foal? You think you can sell them in Oregon?"

"Nah, I intend to stay there. This is my last trip."

"Oh, well, I can see why you want her then. I'm guessing you know more about horses than I do. Can you get a saddle on one of Patty's horses and see if it's gentle enough for her to ride?"

He took the saddle and blanket and rubbed them up against each of her horses and found one that didn't shy away. "This one may have had a saddle at one time." He put the blanket on and eased the saddle over its back. It started to object when he cinched it up and then settled down. Next, he took the rope lead out of its mouth and put the bridle on. The metal bit didn't seem to bother the horse. He led it around for a minute or more, then vaulted onto its back to see a reaction. The horse was fine, so he dismounted and said, "Come on, Patty and see if this ornery animal likes you enough to carry you."

Tom helped her up, and she sat proud and tall for such a small girl. He led her around for a little, then let her have control. The horse responded well as she guided it around the area.

"Okay, I think you have the best horse around. Let it get some rest as we have a big day tomorrow."

Ina helped her off and then removed the saddle. She hobbled it and made sure the others were too. By now, she had rewrapped all the items we had left and set them up for the early morning ride.

"I guess we'll be up with you in the morning, Tom. You better get some sleep."

He left, and we turned in for the night. Patty was excited and had some trouble sleeping. I ventured outside the body and visited her. Her spirit relaxed, and she was asleep in an instant. Ina was taking this in and accepted me for what I was. "You will go soon," she said in her tongue.

"Yes, I will, but not till I finish what I was called for."

She rolled over and went to sleep as if this was the nature of things in her world. Mine was always in flux, and I still didn't know why I was here. No one on the train had been highlighted, so it had to be someone somewhere else. Maybe I can get a handle on the situation at the fort.

Day Ten

It had been a long day and short night, but the body got enough rest to handle it. I wasn't sure if Ina and Patty would be so lucky, but I had them up early to join Tom. He came over to help get the horses lined up and saddled Patty's for her. She was rubbing the sleep out of her eyes and chewing on a piece of jerky. We rode out before the women had breakfast ready, knowing we wouldn't get a meal till the wagon master called a halt late in the day. Everyone else would get a lunch break.

I let Ina ride lead with Tom while I held back to make sure Patty was able to keep up. I had filled the canteen in the river before leaving. It had to last all day, but Tom was carrying one also. The crew of men who kept the trail clear for the wagons would have their breakfast before going out.

I listened while Tom and Ina talked. They didn't seem to be talking to each other but still communicating somehow. There wasn't much to see as we crossed the open prairie, but Tom would stand up in the stirrups and rotate his head back and forth every once in a while. I didn't have that problem as the itch in the back of my head would warn me of trouble, and nothing was happening.

The other conversation going one way was Patty as she talked to her horse. It would flick its ears as she jabbered away. I kept my peace and concentrated on what might lay ahead. Somewhere I had a job to do and couldn't understand why it must be so far out. I might not remember the jobs I did or who I represented, but one thing I did know. I was called to kill someone, and it didn't seem to be anyone on this wagon train. Shooting Indians wasn't it either.

We stopped for lunch, and Ina got out a chunk of buffalo meat and some biscuits she pilfered from one of the cooks. It was a better meal than Tom had expected, as he was carrying jerky and water.

After lunch, I switched with Ina and rode up front with Tom. He had a few questions for me. "Do you care to explain any of this now that we aren't in the vicinity of the rest of this train?"

"Do you think you can handle some really wild information?"

"What you've done is really wild, so I think the answer should be yes."

"Okay. John Vanderwick died out on the trail that night, and I took over his body. I'm known as *The Nomadic Ghost*, a spirit called to perform a service for dead people. John was not one of those calling me."

"I spent a little time in the war and saw lots of odd things take place. I was out early due to a wound suffered during combat. The doctors thought I might never walk again, so they had me discharged. I can walk without the limp when I concentrate on it and riding a horse doesn't create any problems for me. The things I saw while recovering allow me to accept your statement for what you claim."

"Well, it should make the rest of my comments more interesting to you. I think Ina already knows who I am even though she never asked. Now the reason I am called is to remove someone from the living. So far, I haven't been able to determine who it might be, but I don't think he is in this wagon train. When I finish the assignment, I leave the body, and it reverts back to the dead condition it was in when I took it over. If you are around when it happens, you will see John Vanderwick as he was before you gave him the gun."

"So the dead Indians and the horses and Ina and Patty are not the reason you are here?"

"I don't control the circumstances this body lives in. The spirits who call me have just one purpose. It is their responsibility to keep me alive until I accomplish the task they called me for. I have to interact with the people I meet and sometimes use them to benefit those spirits. I can assume the Indians I have killed are not the main reason I'm here, but it could be a side benefit. When I move from one body to the next, I lose most of the memory of what happened."

"Then you don't know who you replaced before taking over for John?"

"Yes and no, as I often have some form of dreams to enlighten me about my past. I have been around since the earliest days of man and the last dream I had showed me as a Confederate soldier."

"Do you know when you were in that body?"

"No, the picture only showed one scene—me taking a shot at someone and being shot for my effort. It didn't show the results of the shot I took, but I have to believe it was successful, or I would have stayed to finish it."

"How will you know when the time comes to eliminate the person or persons?"

"The spirits who want the removal will highlight him or them in some way."

"What would it look like?"

"I will see something marked in red, maybe, as I did the six Indians the first night out. I have a knife that fits the size of the red line on the side of the neck of those Indians. I merely had to insert the knife in the location indicated by them."

"You don't seem to have any emotional response for having killed six men with a knife."

"No, it is one of the things that goes with the territory. By the way, I only killed four of them with the knife; I had to shoot the other two with the gun you gave me. I suppose I should ask whose gun it was and return it."

"No, you keep it. It was mine, and I have another one just like it."

"Maybe the pistol should be worth the price of the filly you want."

"You were right about me not being able to take care of it."

"We can keep it with the others for now. I could hear you and Ina talking but not in the same language. What did you get out of it?"

"Oh, I started by naming a few things, and she got the idea and named them in her language. What does she have to do with the shirt she's wearing?"

I usually notice things of importance and missed that one. I looked back at her and saw the Union Soldiers blue top she had on. "She took it off one of the Indians I killed and seemed to have an attachment to it. When she gets better at speaking English, then you can ask her."

Oregon was still some months away, but I had no idea if Ina planned on going there or if she was just following me till I finished my assignment.

It wasn't long after the lunch break when one of the pioneers rode up. "Hi, my wife sent some food for you. She was worried the little girl might go hungry."

"Oh, that's nice of her," I said. "We did bring some food along, but I bet she could eat some more now."

"My name is Sam, Sam Harding. My wife is Harriet. It seems odd talking to you as if you were her father or something. Everyone knows how bad it got for you before you left us, and I'm apologizing for my family not being more considerate."

"I understand the reason and hold no grudge toward anyone on the wagon train."

"My wife wanted to ask if Patty would like to join us, but we can't take care of her horses."

"You might ask her, but I don't think she will give up those horses. She was very proud of catching them."

"Really, how did she do it?"

"Oh, they were swimming in the river, and when they came out, she grabbed the lead ropes on all four of them. No one saw how she did it, so maybe the horses just went to her. Since the previous owners no longer needed them, they became her property."

We stopped, and Sam gave the food to Ina, who helped Patty get down. We all ate some of the food he brought.

Tom said, "I have work to do," as he munched on a biscuit. He mounted up and rode out to keep checking the route for problems.

Sam said, "There's some problem with the Indian you have with you. Mind you, it's not me but others on the wagon train."

"You wouldn't care to elaborate, would you?"

"The rumor going around has to do with the marks on her."

"Yeah, it is a problem. Ina has had a hard life until now, and someone made sure she would keep having one. I don't see it as a problem for her but for those who might want to blame her for something she had no control over."

"How did she come into your possession?"

"First off, I have no way or means of possessing her. She can do as she pleases. She and Patty were being held captive by some Indians, and when I eliminated them, she willingly joined me. If she

41

wanted to leave, she had not indicated so. She may think she has to protect Patty but hasn't pointed out that either."

"We have a ways to go before we get to Fort Henry. Maybe Patty would like to ride in the wagon with us on some days if you and Ina can take care of her horses."

"That might be a nice break for her and give her a chance to get used to you and Harriet. We'll see how she feels about it when we get in tonight."

Sam started back while Ina, Patty, and I went after Tom. I let Ina catch up to him, and I stayed back with the horses and Patty.

"Patty, I know you heard Mr. Harding talk about you and how he would like for you to ride in his wagon on some days. We're going to be out here for a long time. Do you think you would like that?"

"I want my horses."

"Yes, I know, and they might not be able to take care of them and still get their wagon all the way to Oregon. No one will make you do anything you don't want as long as I'm here, but I don't think I'll get to Oregon, and you might. Ina and I will let you decide what you want to do."

"I want my horses."

"Okay, you have your horses, and we'll see how the rest of it goes."

She went back to talking to her horse, and I went back to thinking about why I might still be out here on the trail. I let everything that happened so far run through the memory bank of this brain and tried to evaluate each thing in turn. The two boys who treated John badly were now dead, and the loss would be felt by their family. Would they have any reason to cause me or Ina trouble? We didn't have anything to do with the boys going outside the wagon compound. The Indians had lost too many braves and were glad to have a reason to stop the attack. The wagon master may have been the reason no one wanted to accept John Vanderwick. He had basically stolen the gold coins from the boy. I didn't tell anyone else about the coins, but would he believe that? I had mentioned money to Tom but not in gold. Could he have said something to anyone else?

I knew most of the riders and some of the pioneers wanted the horses but didn't have anything to trade for them. The horses and other herbivores could eat the grasses growing out here on the prairie, but when we reached the mountains, someone would have to pack feed for them.

I was still thinking about all this when the alarm in the back of my head went off. The itch was light at first but continued to grow. I switched places with Ina and told Tom something was coming our way. About that time, he could see them at a distance. There were four Indians on horseback riding directly toward us.

"I think this is trouble. I have been warned to be careful."

Tom answered, "This is why we send out a lead to check the trail."

I looked back and could see Ina had pulled her rifle out and had the butt of it on her hip. "Looks like Ina is aware of the trouble also."

"She's going to have trouble every time she meets some Indians."

Tom and I made sure our handguns were visible and kept riding until we reached them.

I didn't recognize three of the Indians, but the fourth had a patch where a bullet had gone in. Ina noticed it also and leveled her gun—just in case.

The four of them rode directly into us to make us move apart. Ina refused to let them go between her and Patty. The horses were all tied together, so they couldn't separate them, and they rode on past and then left the trail. We watched as they rode north for a while and turned west.

Tom commented, "They had a muzzle-loader and one handgun. I think they were the ones from the raiding party who attacked us back across the river."

"They are, and the one Ina shot is with them. They don't have any of the rifles, but the muzzle-loader is a big bore gun. They probably used it to shoot buffalo at one time."

We watched them for a while, then I said, "They will be looking for a place to ambush us and maybe shoot the horse out from under you. I'm going out to track them. Go slow for the next mile or two. They will be looking for a good location or already know of one."

"I would tell you to say here because it's dangerous, but you have already proved it's not you who will be in trouble."

"Hey, with any luck, we should have four more ponies in the next couple of hours."

"Yeah? Let me know if any of them are pregnant."

"The Indians or the horses?" That got a smile out of him.

The Indians had dropped out of sight and had no idea I was following them. They had gone into an arroyo and used it to get close to the trail without being seen. It also kept them from seeing me as I entered the gap in the prairie. They had hobbled their horses and walked down the arroyo. I left Army with their horses and cocked the handgun while keeping as quiet as possible.

The one holding the rifle had set up in a prone position to get a shot. That would be at Tom or his horse, of course. The other Indians had placed themselves behind and a little below him in order to stay out of sight until he fired.

He never got the chance as I slipped in behind them without being noticed. The Indian nearest me either heard or felt something and spun around with a bow and arrow. Before he could release it, I pulled the trigger and put a slug in the middle of his torso. The other three were moving fast, and I could see the muzzle of the big gun swing in my direction. It discharged at the same time as my revolver, and he missed me but took my bullet in the head.

I had a little trouble getting the hammer back for another shot when an arrow flew past. It missed me by about an inch or two. He didn't get a second chance as I dropped the hammer on the next round. The fourth Indian had gone down the arroyo a few yards and turned to shoot at me with the handgun, but Tom had reached the area and managed to get a clean shot at him.

Ina had stayed back a little to protect Patty and keep the horses from getting nervous. She got off her horse and collected the weapons. They would be added to our collection of trade goods.

I use the word *our* a lot, but I know I won't be taking anything with me when I leave. I can help get Ina and Patty some things they can use later. We might make it to Fort Henry, where we can trade for those things. I'm still here, so this encounter wasn't why I had been called.

I walked the five horses down the arroyo and added their four to the ones already in tow. "Let's see now, is that thirteen plus four? If these Indians don't stop trying to kill us, we'll have all their horses. Hey, Tom, thanks for the cover shot. I couldn't get this gun cocked fast enough to finish them all off."

"You didn't do all that bad, though. The last Indian said something, but I didn't understand what it was."

Ina spoke up, "Him say, 'Tonto.' "

"What does that mean?"

None of us knew why he said it or if it meant anything.

I said, "It sounded like a name, but they don't use those kinds, do they?"

It was a rhetorical question, and I didn't get an answer. We left the bodies where they ended up and checked the area for other problems and found none. The trail crew would have a little work here where it crosses the arroyo as a summer storm must have pushed debris across it.

We could see a long way across the prairie from here, and Tom called a halt for the day. We were out far enough that the wagon train would probably cross the arroyo and camp for the night. When the road gang got there, Tom had them put some dirt over the bodies to keep from attracting animals overnight.

The word had spread almost as if everyone knew it as soon as it happened. The trail boss asked, "What are you doing to attract those horses to yourself?"

"Gee, Boss, I think the Indians just want to get rid of all these old nags."

The riders and several of the pioneers came around to count and inspect the new trophies. They couldn't tell one from another except where Patty made sure to keep hers away from the on-lookers.

Everyone settled down for the evening and a good meal before it got dark. Sam and Harriet Harding invited Patty to join them and get a look at their schooner. They had four mules pulling it and the horse Sam rode. The horse was tied to the back of the wagon most of the time. They showed Patty where she could tie up her horse if she rode with them, but the other horses would have to stay with the herd. She wasn't happy and told them so.

Sam told me about it later but didn't take offense. He and Harriet found Patty to be refreshingly blunt for a five-year-old. "She must have picked up some of your directness, as has Ina."

"I guess they have, but I can only hope they keep it after I'm gone."

"Where are you going?"

"Oh, I won't be making the trip all the way to Oregon, but as of now, I have no idea where I'll end up. It could be Fort Henry, but I'll have to wait and see."

"What will you do with the horses?"

"I think they can be traded at the fort, and we'll have to get something useful in return."

"I intend to start a store in Portland when we get there. I wanted some of the things you have, but I need the items I'm carrying to open with."

"You can check with Ina and Patty in Fort Henry to see what they have left. I think the horses will bring them enough supplies to finish the trip."

"You seem as if you will be letting them do the dealing."

"Oh, no, I just will probably have other things to do there or close to there and will give them a hand if they need it."

"Everyone wants to know how you changed after leaving the wagon train."

"I'll never be able to explain it to you and the rest. Maybe you can ask Tom Brown when you get to Oregon. He seems to have a handle on it."

"I see him limp a lot. What is that from?"

"He was in the war and got wounded. I think he's lucky to be able to walk at all. The doctors let him out early because of the condition of the leg. He could never march again. He might see it as a handicap of some kind, but I like his character and fortitude."

I left him to think about the things I said and went out to where Ina and Patty had the horses. I was going to need someone to break one of the ponies for me. I knew the fort was run by the army, and they would want Army back. I hoped they didn't get irate over Ina wearing the army jacket. I should try to find out why she thinks so much of it. We still had a few days to go before getting to the fort.

Ina had waited till I got there before settling down, but Patty, with her belly full, wasn't waiting for me or anyone else. She slipped into the dream world and was long gone before Ina and I closed down the night.

I had picked up enough of her language and said, "I want to ask if you have a wish on where to go or if you are here because I have some influence on you?"

"You are a spirit man like the Chief said. I need to be with you till you go back to the spirit world. You have saved my life and helped Patty. Now I help you till you are no more."

"You are very brave and show strength when bad things go on

around you. Many people here and other places will think of you as a bad person. I know it is not of your choosing, and I am glad to have you with me. One day soon, I will be called to go someplace else, and you will have to work out your own future. I can only guess you have lost your tribe forever and will need a new place to be. Maybe it will be in Oregon, but I have heard of a tribe in Walla Walla. You will be close to there and may seek to find a home with them. We will see what happens at Fort Henry and if you can go on from there."

"You think to end at the fort?"

"I have no way of knowing, but it would seem to be the place. We will find out in a few days. You must stick close to Tom, and he will help you when I'm gone. I have to ask about the army shirt you have."

"Yes, it was on a soldier who tried to protect me."

"The fort has more army people there, and they might ask about the shirt or try to take it from you."

"I can hide it when we are there."

With that, I called it a night, rolled up in a blanket, and set the body in sleep mode.

Sleep is not always peaceful for me, as the wagon train of my past will haunt me from time to time. The word Tonto showed up, and the spirits who called me let me know it was all right. They didn't indicate, bad or not, as they slid the past backward to show the evolution of the killer I had become. I was always a male of youthful vigor and able to fight with any type of weapon. When I would slay the intended target, I would be called to another body. Each new body was in distress as the spirit in it was leaving. I sometimes had to push it out of the way to gain access.

Why would you torment me with things I cannot change? The images of blood and guts floated through my eternal vision. I was aware those who call me don't always have the best interests of society in mind. Vengeance or retribution is more to their liking. This would be no different than a thousand or more before it. I saw to the demise of kings and queens of paupers and pirates, none of which followed me on this endless run.

This body relaxed as the pictures mellowed to show the times when I might have been allowed to enjoy the company of the opposite sex. I would find the riches of barons and squires in the arms of the women they had. All could be influenced by the youthful exuberance I could show them. Even at that, I failed sometimes and had to be called back to finish what was asked of me. I became less emotional after each failure and now find it hard to share the joy and passion of the present.

I have been charged with the need to protect Ina and Patty from any violence, yet I cannot bring this body to feel their pain or joy. Were they for me or for the ghosts who call me? They might profit from the things I do, but someone else will have the benefit of their company when I am gone.

Days on End

The rest of the trip to Fort Henry was clouded by routine and boredom. Ina stayed away from the pioneers but had a constant interchange of conversation with Tom. They both had defects and were learning to ignore them when they rode together. I spent more time with Patty and the horses. I worked with one of them to see if I could get it trained without help. I, *The Nomadic Ghost*, connected with him until he would let me get on him without a saddle or bridle. It took only two days to train him to a saddle with this method. He was a "horse of a different color" of a breed I wasn't aware of, and I called him Paint. He had been the one attracting most of the attention from the riders and the pioneers. Most of the horses were brown or brown and white, with one being grey. He looked old because of the color, and no one was interested in him.

I noticed Tom and Ina were spending more time together, and Patty was getting to like the Harding couple. To fill the time, I worked with the horses and had most of them trained to the saddle. All of them had been ridden before, so it was just the cinch and new weight they had to get used to. Once I had managed to get Paint trained, then the others were much easier. I only had a few hours each night to work with them but would ride a different one the next day. I left the grey horse till last and found him to be quite nice to ride.

One Day to the Fort

We camped on the prairie with the knowledge we would be stopping at the fort soon. The wagon master announced, "We're about a half-day out from the fort. You may want to go through your things and see what you might need for the next segment of the trip. We'll get an early start tomorrow and set up camp outside the fort when we get there. I sent a rider ahead to let them know we were coming. I think we might have to spend three days there, as several wagons need repairs and the animals need a break. The Conestogas are holding up better than the prairie schooners, but the oxen are slowing a bit. We're a little behind schedule due to the Indian raid, but it won't be a problem with the weather as it's been unusually dry this trip."

The Hardings' wagon needed some repairs as the weight they were hauling was taking its toll. Patty had spent a little more time with them but was still adamant about keeping her four horses. No one else would even talk about them. The repairs and rest were needed, as the ground would get more mountainous from there on out.

I had noticed Tom and Ina were spending more time together but being discreet about it. Patty had grown to like the Hardings, and I had gotten familiar with the horses. All of that left me with the feeling something was missing. What was I doing here? Did this set of ghosts forget what they called me to do? Memory is a fleeting thing for those of us in the spectral world. Maybe Fort Henry was the destination, as I was having trouble thinking past it.

Most of the people on the wagon train knew I had broken the

Indian ponies to the saddle and bridle but had no idea how I did it. They would see me riding a different horse each day, including the grey one. I even broke Patty's other three, but all the horses needed their toenails trimmed. I guess they might get shoes at the fort or have to wait until this train got to Portland. There are several more forts along the way, but I think I'll not see them.

This night was different from all the rest of those I've had on this trip. The ghosts wanted me to know something important. The image of one riding a grey horse and leading a painted one and a pack mule came visibly to mind as the body slept. The mountains rose up ahead of this rider along a path lighted in red. The Henry .44 was hanging in a leather scabbard off the right side, and the S & W pistol was holstered off the left. The pack animal had items of need for a long journey, but the feeling was short-lived. Someone else would need the things the mule carried. Then the dream state reverted back to the past of this assassin as the number of bodies mounted. I would have to endure the assault on this brain even though it had never seen such mayhem before. John Vanderwick was young and inexperienced but the spirit now driving his body was not. The glimpses into the past showed how easy it was to remove the living and add them to the never-ending list. Each time, I would see the glow of the spirit leave for its next destination, though I had no idea where it would be. I was not privileged to join them but kept answering the call for more blood. The night ended, and a new day dawned with the muscle cramps of clenched fists.

Fort Henry

Everyone ate a quick meal, started to assemble the teams, and pack the overnight things. I had help from Ina as we got all our gear on the horses and headed out to catch up to Tom. He skipped the meal and was making sure the route was clear again. He had taken on the job as if he owned it, but that would change in a few days. Patty tied her horse to the Harding wagon and climbed on board for the ride. They were glad to have her as she chatted away. Sam had said, "It made the day go faster."

We weren't going to catch Tom before he got to the fort. We were interrupted by incoming riders who had heard about the horses we might have. I wondered how they found out about them but failed to ask. I had forgotten the wagon master had sent someone ahead to let them know we were coming. There were four of them, and they looked over the herd for the best ones. I was riding the grey, and Ina was on Paint, as she wanted to give her horse a break from carrying her. The four newcomers must have been warned about Ina, as they gave her room to get by even though they would have liked to get a closer look at Paint.

I said, "We will discuss the horses tomorrow when we see what they can be traded for."

One of them asked, "How did you get hold of so many horses?"

Ina answered, "He kill lots of Indians and take them."

They must not have heard it from the rider but only that we had some. Ina had taken her rifle and held the butt against her thigh again as if to protect the horses and me.

They weren't going to argue with her over it but seemed to be a little skeptical. I said, "The three in that line are owned by someone in the wagon train, and the one with the Army brand came from the band of Indians who attacked the wagon train."

"Are you holding these for some adult?"

"No, my partner here just told you how they come into my possession, and I will be the one to trade them off tomorrow at the fort."

"Are you going to take currency for any of them?"

"No, I might take gold or silver, but only if I can't get trading goods instead. I'm not sure the currency is any good now or if it can be used in the Oregon territory."

They rode with us the rest of the way but maintained a distance from Ina and her Henry .44.

Tom was waiting for us with some information. "They have wagons and mules here from a previous wagon train that had an outbreak of stomach problems. Forty people got sick, and twelve died." He helped us stake out the horses a little way from where the army wanted the wagons parked.

We separated the six horses that were not to be traded. They would be the two from my dream state, Ina's, and the three owned by Patty. It still left almost a dozen available. It was more than I could count on both hands. The word was put out that we would wait till morning and see what was in the fort we might need or use.

The army sergeant setting up the campground area noticed Army the horse and motioned for me to remove it from the herd. He continued to help with the setup and then took the horse when he returned to the fort. A captain came out with the sergeant and asked, "Where did you get the army horse?"

"The wagon train was attacked by a band of Indians. They had him and all the rest of these horses. Once they didn't need them anymore, I took possession of them."

He looked at me. "You don't look big enough or old enough to claim anything from a band of Indians."

Tom stepped in. "Don't let the size fool you any. He has done as he says, and some of us got to see it happening."

"Okay, I'll take your word for it. Now the horse with the brand on it belongs to the army, and we are taking it back."

"I didn't argue with the sergeant, and I won't argue with you over it. I was sure it would be reclaimed and took it into consideration. Now there must be a finder's fee for returning lost items, and he was definitely lost when we got hold of him."

"I'll take it up with the major when I go back in."

He then made the rounds of the camp and talked to the trail boss and several others. Sam Harding stopped him to ask, "I need some work done on my prairie schooner. Do you have a smithy here?"

"Yeah. What do you need?"

"I think the rims are starting to break loose."

"I'll have him look at it tomorrow. He'll be out here to look at the horses, mules, oxen, and anything else the trail boss thinks of."

We settled down and got something to eat, after which I indicated Ina should watch the horses while Tom and I went into the fort to have a look around. They had four prairie schooners and twenty mules, and they wanted them out of there. The mules would be turned into dinner unless someone took them away.

The army supplied the forts with provisions and those things most needed on the trail. The store was run by a private owner, and he reimbursed the army for delivering the items he requested. Food supplies, tools, and bullets, in that order, were what went first. The fort also had a blacksmith for repairs and maintenance. We checked for all the things we might need, and I asked Tom, "Do you expect Ina to go to Oregon with you?"

"We haven't gotten that far yet, but it might be a possibility."

"I think this is as far as I'm going with the wagon train. I'll need some supplies, a mule, the grey horse, and Paint. I'm being called for a trip to the mountains."

"How will you keep Ina and Patty from going with you?"

"I'll have to let them know it is something only I can do. Patty will have to get someone to take her horses. I'm pretty sure the Hardings would like to have her stay with them. We have a couple of days to work things out."

We were headed to see the blacksmith and ran into Sam. "I need to see if the smithy can get the wheel rims to last longer. I didn't expect the weight to cause this much damage, and we have the mountains to cross yet."

I thought about it for a split second and said, "Why not get another wagon and split the load?"

"I can't handle two at the same time, and Harriet can't even do one of them."

"Well, we have some time to work things out, and the mules will be slaughtered if no one takes them. They don't want to keep feeding them with the limited supply they have now."

We stopped at the smithy's, and Sam asked, "My rims are working loose, and I might need something more heavy-duty. What have you got?"

"Sorry, we have a limited supply here of rims, and they are all the same. You must have a heavy load, and it happens all the time. People end up throwing stuff out to make it through the mountains. I'll have a look at them tomorrow and see what can be done. Now, what can I do for you?" he said while looking at Tom.

"I'm just along for the ride. John, here, owns several horses, and they might need some work."

He turned to me and asked, "How many do you have?"

"I think about a dozen or so. They're Indian ponies, and the hooves will need some trimming."

"Oh, your reputation has preceded you. I wasn't expecting one so young or small to have so many ponies."

"I'll be trading the majority of them off for things I need. Two of mine will need shoes, and one more will need to be checked. It has shoes, but they may have been put on some time ago."

"We can look at them tomorrow and get an idea of what can be done. Sometimes the Indian ponies get bad feet and lower leg problems if not taken care of. I have two apprentices, and they will be out there with me."

"How did you end up with two apprentices out here?"

"Just take a look at the wagons sitting out there."

"Oh, part of the twelve who didn't make it."

He didn't elaborate, and I let it go. "I'll see you in the morning."

Tom and I joined Sam as he was walking out. "What do you have in the wagon that makes it so heavy?"

"We will be opening a store in Portland, and I have items useful for cutting timber. They are in high demand right now, so I really need to get them over the mountains."

"I know you don't think much of the horses Patty has, but you might want to give a thought to using them to transport some of your tools. They have been used as pack animals before."

"I'll have to think on it. Taking care of animals gets harder with each one you add to your inventory. Replacing the tools with horse feed might not reduce the weight much."

We left him to ponder his dilemma and went to see how Ina was coping with the interested horsemen.

I used her language and asked her, "How are you doing with the horses?"

"There are many men but no trade goods."

"Yeah, I knew it might be a problem."

"You talk to smith?"

"Yes, he will be out in the morning and has two helpers."

"Which horses we keep and not keep?"

"I need Grey and Paint. You keep yours and have the shoes checked or replaced. Tom keeps the filly he picked out."

"How we pay smith?"

"I'll see tomorrow what he will take."

Tom was taking all this in and trying to keep up. He hadn't gotten as far as I had on her language but got some of it. "What are you doing with the filly I want?"

"I told her to keep it for you, but you will have to see about the hooves and if it needs shoes now. You might ask if you should wait till she drops the foal. You'll be in Portland by then."

Ina hadn't bothered to set out the other stuff and asked, "You want try trade these things?" She pointed to the bundle holding things we accumulated from the Indians.

I thought the bow and arrow sets might draw some interest. There were a few of those, and we had the hatchet/tomahawks. The baubles, beads, and mirrors might be useful here. I thought we could donate the extra items to Sam for his store if we couldn't get anything for them.

Tom went into the camp and got a couple of plates of food for him and Ina.

Patty was with her horses, and I took her away from them. "Let's go get something to eat. Ina will watch your horses."

"I want my horses," she said.

"I know, Patty. Maybe we can work something out so you can get them to Oregon with you."

She had gotten into the bundle of trinkets and had six sets of beads around her neck. "Do you like the beads?" I asked.

"No, I want to sell them."

"What do you want to sell them for?"

"I want food for my horses."

"Good thinking there. Your horses could carry their own food with them."

"They are strong, so I can get lots of food for them."

I wasn't sure she could pull it off, but she had done okay to this point.

Several people came by to look at the horses again, and Ina watched to make sure nothing was bothered. Word had gotten around that she could use the Henry rifle.

The sergeant came back and brought the major with him. They came over to me, and the major asked, "Are you the runt claiming these horses?"

"My name is John Vanderwick, and if you keep calling me names, we can get a two-way contest going."

"Well, John Vanderwick, I guess I had it coming. I've been informed you own these horses, and if I want any of them, I might have to talk to you about them."

"We will be open for trading them in the morning and see what the smithy says about their feet."

"I could just requisition them from you and give you a paymaster's letter so you can collect from the U. S. Army."

"You're the only army I've seen, and I don't expect to be in contact with any more armies for a while. If you hold something of value, we can trade for the horses you want."

"Well, we had a little problem and lost six horses. Now I need to replace them somehow."

"Why don't you come back in the morning and we can discuss our needs? I'm sure we can make an arrangement that works for both of us."

"I'll do that, but you can't let anyone take them before I get out here."

I watched him walk off and thought, "This might be too easy. He lost six horses, and I have seven that need to go. Most of the pioneers and riders couldn't or wouldn't pay for them in tradable wear."

We turned in for the night, and I, *The Nomadic Ghost*, started to formulate a plan. I would have to take it up with Tom and Ina in the morning.

The body went to sleep, and the spirit sat in on another trip, but this one was futuristic. I was again riding on Grey and leading Paint and a pack mule. The scene showed the prairie in the background and the mountains ahead. Why was I needed in the mountains? The purpose became clear as I saw six riders headed north. Four of them were bathed in red. I had been called here to remove them, and it was up in the mountains of the Wyoming Territory.

Daybreak

Ina was up and about as soon as she saw me move. I had a question for her which would lead to more of them. "I see you and Tom spending time together. Do you think you will go to Oregon with him?"

"He has not asked me."

"Will you go with him if he asks you?"

"Yes."

Direct questions get direct answers. "I'll speak to him."

A couple of minutes later, I had Tom over a barrel. "I need to know if you are expecting to take Ina to Oregon with you."

"Why do you need to know? Don't you think she should know first?"

"Tom, I explained it before. I have been called here for a reason, and you and Ina are not it. Patty isn't in the picture here either. I'll be leaving the wagon train in the next day or two and may not see any of you again. Ina has been focused on protecting me once I shared the buffalo heart with her and Patty. Now I have something to do, and it will probably end this body's life."

"I have to believe you but find it difficult. You have been a part of our lives for a month or more. I know you don't have a choice, but making us choose is not fair."

"If you don't want her with you, then you must tell her, as she will try to follow me even if I tell her not to."

"I will ask her now, as I do want her with me."

Ina was busy setting out the trade goods while I took Patty over to get something to eat. I talked to her about the Hardings. "Do you like Sam and Harriet?"

"Yes, but they don't want my horses."

"Did you sell some beads yesterday?"

"No one wants them."

"I think Ina and Tom are going to Oregon, and I will ask them to help you with the horses."

"Oh, thank you."

By the time we got back from breakfast, several people had inquired about the horses. I stated, "The major is interested in the horses and told me not to trade any until he sees them. I'm sorry, but he runs the fort here and gets first choice."

The blacksmith was making the rounds of the pioneers and their wagons, and I expected him to visit me last as we were outside the perimeter of the camp. It all changed when the major came out to look at the horses. He ordered the sergeant, "Go get the blacksmith for me."

I could see he was used to giving orders and knew they would be followed. He looked at me. "The smith knows his animals and will give me a good report on the ones you have here. I know you want something from me in exchange for the horses and for bringing back the branded one. So what do you want that I might have?"

"You have wagons and mules, and I need two and nine in that order."

"What will you do with two wagons?"

"One of our wagons is carrying too much weight, and the mules for it are worn out. If we split the load in two, then they may get to Oregon. Also, I need two horses and a mule. The horse with shoes belongs to Ina the Indian. The three horses over there belong to Patty, the little girl. I can explain all of it if you like. That leaves seven horses if I count them right."

"I'll take those seven as soon as the smith checks them out. Now, why do you need the extra mule and two horses?"

"I'm going after your six missing horses. The mule is to carry some supplies so I won't go hungry if it takes a while to catch up to them."

"I can't stop you but suggest it's not a good idea. We sent out a six-man patrol to bring them back, but the bandits ambushed my men, and I lost two and had two more wounded. They shot two of those horses also."

"Does that mean they are not running but waiting you out?"

"I don't know what their intentions are, but they took two women with them. I hoped to get them back alive."

"So tell me about the men. How many and what kinds of weapons do they have?"

"I'll give you the long story but cut it short. There were six men on the wagon train when it got here, and everyone was sick with dysentery. Two of those men died, and the four recovered. We didn't know at the time, but they joined the wagon train just before it got here. They surprised the guards and took supplies and those horses along with the two women. They are armed with the same kind of rifles you have but didn't have any munitions for them. They stole about a hundred rounds along with the other supplies. I'm shorthanded here as the Indian tribes to our east have been causing trouble, and I had to send some men back there."

"Thank you for the information. I will still need the horses and mule and supplies enough for two weeks. If I manage to get your horses back, then I might want mine. In the meantime, you get to use them and don't need to send out more troops."

Tom had been taking all this in and watched to see the reaction from the major. "I think the major is just playing a game with you to see how far you might go."

"Oh, he might think of it as a game, but those four men I'll be after will next appear in the hereafter."

"You don't intend to bring them back to stand trial?" the major asked.

"You might want to ask the horses if I brought any of their riders back to face a jury of their peers."

"I'm still working off the rumors and have a lot of trouble believing in them."

"That's okay; when your horses get back, you can ask the two women how it happened."

The smithy finished checking all the horses and proclaimed them good except for the hooves.

I asked, "Do the grey and the dappled horse need shoes or hooves trimmed?"

"It would depend on how hard they will be ridden. I think the hooves should be trimmed anyway, but if you intend to ride either of them, then they should have shoes put on. Now, what are you two talking about?"

The major answered, "We were dickering over how many supplies I'm willing to give him for the horses."

"If he gives me the two wagons and nine mules, then you won't have to fix the Harding unit."

"Are they going to move their stuff to another wagon?"

"That was the idea."

"It'll still be too heavy."

"That's what the second one is for. If we cut the weight in half and bring in fresh mules, it should be an easier trip the rest of the way."

"Who's going to ride the second wagon?"

"I'm still working on it."

"I've been trying to get rid of those mules, so giving you nine of them is easy, but the wagons could bring some money," the major said.

"I'll talk to the Hardings about it and see what they have to say. I'm sure their wagon won't make it even if it's repaired here."

The smith agreed. "Yeah, the trail gets a little rougher for the next month or more."

"I'll throw in the wagons if you buy your own supplies," the major offered.

"I'll see how it works out."

The major said, "Sergeant, gather up those seven horses and get them into the fort. We can have them shod after the wagon train leaves. Okay, son, you live with it, or I just take the horses."

"I got it, Captain."

He nearly burst out laughing, but the sergeant couldn't contain himself and did a poor job of hiding it. "That's enough, sergeant," the major ordered. "Smithy, put shoes on his two horses before you do anything for the rest of the train. Then get the wagons and mules out here for this runt." The sergeant burst out laughing again as he pulled the ropes on the seven horses.

Tom stood there looking at me. "Now what do we do?"

"Did you get a response from Ina?"

"Yes, she's going with me."

"Good. Now I need to find out if she will handle the second wagon for the Hardings." She had been behind me, and I knew it but didn't let on.

"Yes, I can do that."

"I think riding a horse and leading the mules will be easier than sitting in a bucking wagon. Harriet did a lot of walking as we came across the prairie, and it's probably going to get rougher from here on in. I'll go tell the Hardings what we plan on doing."

Sam was sitting next to his wagon and munching on a piece of jerky. "Hi, John. What are you up to?"

"I just got done talking to the major and secured a wagon for you. In fact, I got two of them. The smithy thinks he can fix yours, but it won't last all the way to Portland."

"Do you think a different wagon will last any longer than the one I have now?"

"Yeah, as I think we can get half of your load in one and the other half in the second one. Ina thinks she can handle the second one for you and get our extra stuff in with it."

"Why would you do that?"

"We need a compromise. You have to help Patty with her horses, and we help you get to Portland with all your tools and supplies."

"That's taking on a bunch with all your horses and hers."

"Oh, I traded the horses for the wagons and got two sets of mules. Now, all we need to do is outfit for the rest of the trip."

"How many horses are we talking about?"

"Let's see, four for Patty and one for Ina, yours and maybe Tom's. You'll need to bag some grain for them and the mules to supplement the prairie grasses they will eat. I'm guessing the mountain area might not have much in the way of grass, but I could be wrong."

"You didn't mention your horse."

"I won't be going with you from here."

"Are you going to stay here?"

"No, I have other plans and will be leaving in the next day or so."

"You willing to talk about it?"

"Yes and no. I have a mission to accomplish, and the major knows why. I probably won't see any of you again as I don't intend to go to Oregon."

"What do I do about Patty?"

"She likes you. She might end up with Tom and Ina if it gets too complicated for you and Harriet."

"We can't have any kids, and Harriet would love to have Patty stay with us."

"What, that spoiled brat? You might be sorry because she is headstrong and demanding."

"Harriet loves her and will spoil her some more."

I left him there to ponder the situation and hoped for the best for all concerned. For me, it was the end of the line, and I really didn't feel any sympathy for them. My sympathy must have died many centuries ago.

I stopped and got Tom before going into the fort. "We need supplies, so let's see what they have available in the store."

"I don't have any money yet. We get paid at the end of the trip."

"I have the money from my trip, as the boss returned it. We'll see how far it will go."

The store was well stocked with utensils they got off the abandoned wagons. Tom wouldn't need any, but I might while tracking down the four killers.

"We need to stock some grub, coffee, and grain. The horses and mules might not find enough grass to live. Get a bottle of alcohol in case of sickness."

I let the storekeeper tally each item as we dropped it on the counter. I knew how much the gold was worth, but John Vanderwick had no idea. He would have died, and the wagon master would have had the gold. As it was, the items we bought were worth only half the amount I had. John's parents would never know how well he did after dying.

By the time we got back, the wagons and mules were there waiting for us. I had Sam take his wagon out of the line and park it next to them. I let him and Tom move the boxes of tools and other items, and they guessed what would make an even load for each wagon. We then took one of them into the fort to pick up the supplies I had already paid for. We made it look like Tom was running everything until it got to the money.

Harriet had tried talking with Ina and soon found a few words they both knew. Over the next months on the trail, they would learn even more. Patty helped with some of the translations and pushed Ina to learn more English.

Both my horses would be ready in the morning.

Tom said, "You don't show much in the way of emotion, but you do have a sense of humor from time to time. Are you anxious about leaving in the morning?"

"No. I know what to expect and will get some help along the way. You need to know this body is dead and has been for a while. I just use it until I finish what they called me for."

"It's so hard to look at you and understand. We people don't have the ability to ignore everything or sometimes anything, just like the major almost laughing about you missing his rank and calling you a runt. The sergeant wasn't able to control the need to laugh. One last question, and I won't ask anymore. Do you know where you go from here?"

"No, it's always a surprise, and I'm usually a full-grown man. Since I can't remember much of my past, I have no way of knowing more. The dreams—or more like nightmares—don't reveal anything about the characters I have been but only the deeds I have done. Most of the time, I must require the physical attributes of a young adult male."

"I'll help you load up in the morning."

"Where did Ina go?"

"She took some things to the store to trade. I'm not sure what she intended to get, but the bows and arrows are things that could sell."

Ina came back with an armful of stuff and handed me a scabbard for my rifle. "You no need carry in hand."

It looked just like the one from the dream state. "Thank you, Ina. I will get good use of it."

The night was on us quickly, and we bedded down. Patty had taken to sleeping with the Hardings, and Ina spent her nights with Tom. Harriet would talk Sam into keeping Patty's horses so she could have Patty stay with them. Ina would help with the horses and the mules, and I knew they would never forget John Vanderwick, but also never really know *The Nomadic Ghost*. The dreams of past lives came again to haunt me or reassure me of who I am.

Breaking Camp

Ina and Tom helped me assemble the items and pack them on the mule. The two horses were brought out by one of the apprentices, and the saddle put on Grey. The rifle was fully loaded and dropped into the scabbard. I checked the cylinder of the pistol for spent rounds and found none. We ate a hearty breakfast, and I mounted up. The major came out to see me off and wish me luck. I rode off without looking back, as I had someplace to go and something to do. The long wait was over as the trail in front of me glowed a light color of red. Those who brought me now led the way.

It was a long ride, taking the best part of three days before I started to get indications of trouble. I came across a long open mesa before ascending into a rocky section of the lower mountains. I expected to camp before going any higher. The feeling of being watched crept into me. The fear of animals is minimal as they tend to fear me due to the ghostly part. But despite that, I could feel the eyes on me. The area around me began to glow a deeper red, and I felt the push to abandon my horse. I leaned forward as the bullet passed me, and I rolled off and fell to the opposite side from where the shot came. I took the pistol with me as I fell and held onto the rein. The horse shielded me from the shooter. He would have to shoot the horse or come down to see if he had hit me.

His recognition of my size would lend him to be less cautious and more risk-taking. The sight of two horses and a pack mule made it seem like an opportunity rather than a gamble. He still used the surrounding vegetation to keep from getting into the open.

When he could see me lying prone behind the horse, he came

closer to make sure of my demise. By the time he recognized movement on my part, the bullet was on its way. He toppled over backward and lay still, and I watched the veiled ghost leave his body and rush off to its next destination.

I reached out with my friends to see if the other three men were anywhere near and found the space around me was now empty of humans. I had an indication of them being higher up in the hills but moving as if to look for some advantage. I picked up the rifle from the dead man and led the horses across the hill to the trees for cover.

It was getting late enough now that the sun was setting; it would be dark shortly. This would give me a benefit beyond anything the other three men could understand. They would have no idea what had happened to their partner since he didn't respond to their calls. The two distinctly different gunshot sounds would indicate bad news, as the second one was not a rifle shot. They had retreated to a safe distance where they might have a clear view of who might be coming after them.

I sat down, took a piece of jerky, and washed it down with a little water from the canteen. I only had to wait a few minutes for it to be dark enough to go looking for them. I popped the spent cartridge out of the cylinder and replaced it with a fresh one. Then I cocked the rifle to ensure a live round was in the chamber. Both guns were now ready when I needed them.

I used the red line provided for me and followed it up the mountain. When I stopped and looked for the men, I could see three red dots a little higher up. They weren't going to get much sleep now, since they expected trouble. They had chosen the location well, and it would have served the purpose except for the time of night. I guessed it would take an hour or more of walking in the dark to get to where they were, but I wasn't in a hurry. It would just give them time to get tired from the tension.

I could smell the smoke long before I could see the fire. It gets cold at night in the mountains, and I had a little trouble understanding why they chose to go there. The three men weren't near the fire but spaced along a ridge to cover the trail coming up from below. I didn't take that route and managed to come in behind the two on the west side. I put the stock of the rifle against a tree and leveled it at the closest man. The shot was going to cause chaos, and the pistol would put a stop to some of it. The little red dot appeared in the middle of his back as I cradled the gun in the crook of my left arm. A light pull on the trigger didn't cause the rifle to move, but the recoil did.

I dropped the rifle, grabbed the pistol, which I knew was already cocked, and held it in both hands. The subject was moving, but the little red dot kept finding him, and the pistol jumped up and almost hit me in the face as I was leaning over it. Both shots were remarkably accurate, and I watched the two spirits depart to places unknown.

The third man was screaming at the top of his lungs to get the attention of his fellow bandits. He was never going to get a response and panicked into grabbing one of the horses and trying to get away. It was dark, and the horse lost its footing on the downhill run and spilled the rider before rolling over him.

Both the animal and rider were screaming in pain as I walked down to help end the noise they were making.

He saw me coming, a little boy with a large handgun. "Help me; I think my horse broke some bones when he rolled over me."

"Yeah, he broke a leg too when you tried to get him running downhill in the dark."

I stuck the muzzle of the pistol in the ear of the horse and pulled the trigger. It stopped the noise from the horse, but the rider was still hollering about the amount of pain he was in.

"Are you going to help me?"

"I'll stop the pain here, but first, I would like to know why the four of you came up here instead of going over the trail."

"You can see the trail from the far side, and we were waiting for the next wagon train to get that far."

"What did you plan to do with the women?"

He seemed to understand his predicament at that point and just begged for help.

I used both hands to cock the pistol and leveled it at him. "You and your friends have caused a lot of trouble. I don't think it's worth my while to try dragging you back to the fort." He screamed as the hammer fell on the next cartridge, and the exploding round covered his last comments.

I walked down to where I left my horses and mule and slowly rode back to their campsite. The women were wrapped in a blanket as close to the fire as they could get.

"Hi, my name is John Vanderwick, and I have been sent to rescue you."

They looked dumbfounded—almost as if they had lost the use of their voices.

"Tomorrow, take the horses and go down to the fort. Another wagon train will be coming through in a couple days. You can hook up with them to get to Oregon. Keep the two horses I brought here along with the mule. They are paid for."

They still couldn't bring themselves to say anything.

"Gather up all the items of value, the guns and ammo and anything you think you might need or can use. I don't think it's worth the effort to bury any of the men. The mule has some supplies, so you can make coffee and fry some salt pork if you are hungry. I have someplace to go, so you need not look for me."

I dropped the handgun and walked away. There was a place high on the mountain that seemed to fit the occasion. I stood and looked out into the predawn sky and asked, "Where to next?" Another set of ghosts were calling me as the body dropped away.

THE END

Other Books by Larry Danek

Jed's World
a science fiction novel

The following books are all part of
The Nomadic Ghost *series and include:*

I'm the Ghost in this Body

Ghostly Reunion

Runaway Ghost

Ghost at the Border

All the above titles are available on Amazon and at select outlets in the Spokane area.

Coming soon:
the next *Nomadic Ghost* adventure